The Umbrella's Story

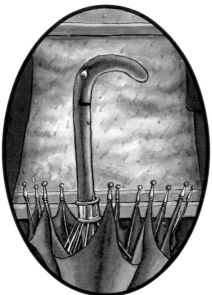

Jez Alborough

LONDON • VICTOR GOLLANCZ LTD • 1988

One blustery spring morning the new umbrella at Featherby House heard a pattering sound outside the front door.

"What's that?" she asked the umbrella stand.

"It's water falling from the sky," he replied. "That's what they call rain and your job is to shelter Mr Featherby from it with your hood, just like the big brown brolly did before you."

"I see," said the new umbrella. "But what happened to the big brown brolly? Where is he now?"

A small gust of wind rattled through the letter-box and the stand looked uneasy.

"The big brown brolly," he solemnly declared, "was taken by a storm."

"A storm," said the new umbrella, "what's that?"

"When the wind howls a ghostly lament and the rain falls so hard that it hammers on the door; when the sky turns as black as coal and rumbles and rages with flashes of anger . . . *that* is a storm," explained the stand.

The new umbrella listened, spellbound, as the stand continued.

"There was a storm on the day last week that the big brown brolly disappeared. Mr Featherby took him to work in the morning, but in the evening . . . he returned alone."

Just then the mantel clock in the dining room struck eight o'clock, and Mr and Mrs Featherby hurried into the hall — Mr Featherby was late for work. As he was helped into his raincoat, he noticed some grey clouds gathering in the sky.

"Looks like a storm is brewing, my dear," said Mr Featherby, and the stand flinched as he bent down to pick up the new umbrella.

Tip-tap-tap, rattled the letter-box while Mr Featherby said goodbye to his wife. He opened the door and the stand bade a tearful farewell to his new friend.

"Oh no," he sobbed. "Now the storm will take you, too."

"Please don't worry," said the new umbrella thoughtfully. "I've a feeling there may be nothing to fear."

Mr Featherby ran panting for the train that was already pulling into the station, and soon the new umbrella found herself hanging from the luggage rack in a crowded carriage. A door slammed, a whistle blew, and the train creaked gently forward. Looking round, the new umbrella noticed several older-looking brollies with their owners, and she was reminded of the big brown brolly.

"Storms can't be *that* bad," she thought, "for surely some of these umbrellas must have been caught in storms, too, yet they are still here serving their owners. Perhaps the storm didn't take the big brown brolly; but then I wonder where he could be now?"

The train hissed slowly into the station. There was pandemonium as all the travellers tried to leave at the same time. Within minutes the carriage was empty, except for a few crumpled newspapers, an unclipped ticket and one new umbrella swinging from the luggage rack. She had been forgotten.

Before long, however, the guard spotted her there and carried her to a dark little office at the back of the station.

"Yet another one," he joked, passing his find to the clerk behind the desk.

The new umbrella was dumped in a dirty tea chest with two other brollies, one large and one small.

"Where am I?" she asked. "What am I doing here?"

"This is the Lost Property Office," said the large brolly, "and you're lost property."

"How clever of you to get yourself lost on a day like this," said the small brolly. "Now you'll miss the storm."

"Is there going to be a storm?" asked the new umbrella, but there was no reply. Both brollies were staring fearfully at the black clouds hovering in the sky.

"When I was lost last week there was a storm," said the large brolly. "It was horrifying. The wind was so strong that it almost wrenched me from my Master's grip. I feared that I would be blown away for ever."

"But you weren't, were you?" insisted the new umbrella. "Otherwise you wouldn't be here now."

The large brolly ignored her and continued with his story.

"The rain began to fall harder and harder until it drummed down on my hood with such force that I felt certain I would be torn to shreds."

Although it was dark in the office, the new umbrella could see that his hood was not ripped at all.

"But the most frightening thing," continued the large brolly, "was nearly being burnt alive . . ."

"Burnt alive!" exclaimed the new umbrella in disbelief. "What happened?"

"There was an ominous rumbling which seemed to be coming closer all the time," said the large brolly. "Then, just as we were climbing into the train, a terrifying BANG shook the sky, and jagged tongues of fire streaked down towards myself and Mr F . . ."

Just then, in a howl of wind and splatter of rain, the office door flew open and in came . . . Mr Featherby.

"I've been found," cried the new umbrella happily.

Suddenly a streak of lightning cracked through the sky, for an instant flooding the dark little office with brilliant light. For the first time the new umbrella could see clearly the colour of the large brolly.

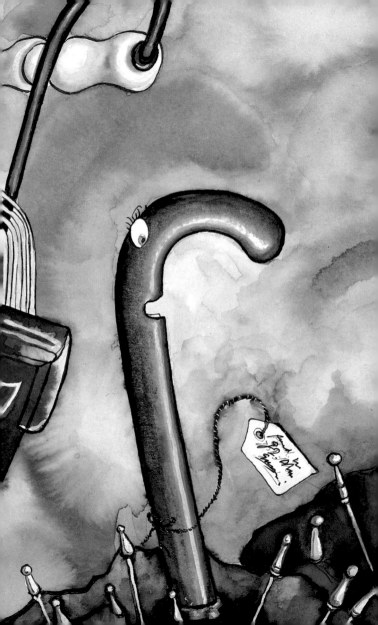

"You're brown! It's you, isn't it? You're Mr Featherby's big brown brolly!" cried the new umbrella.

The big brown brolly gasped. "But how did you know?"

"Because I'm the umbrella Mr Featherby bought to replace you when you went out into that storm last week and never came back. But the storm didn't take you. You weren't blown away, ripped apart or burnt alive, were you? Tell me what *did* happen that day?"

And the big brown brolly told her.

"As the train neared the station the bangs in the sky became even louder. By the time we arrived I was so frightened that, in the rush to leave the carriage, I hid myself beneath the seat. Mr Featherby had to leave without me."

At that moment the clerk gestured towards the tea chest and the big brown brolly quickly shuffled behind his companions, hiding himself from Mr Featherby's view.

"Don't you *want* to be found?" asked the new umbrella incredulously, as the clerk started towards them and the thunder boomed outside.

"It's safe and warm here," explained the small brolly, "and we never have to get wet."

The clerk picked up the new umbrella, and in a flash of lightning she saw clearly her two fellow brollies. She knew then that she would rather face the storm than end up like them, crumpled and cowering in a dirty tea chest.

Mr Featherby was delighted to have found his new umbrella, especially in view of the seasonal downpours. He opened up her hood and locked it into place. She heard the wind howling, the rain hammering on the door and the sky rumbling. She felt frightened, but mixed with her fear was a sense of wonder and excitement.

The new umbrella took a deep breath as Mr Featherby pulled open the door, held her up above his head and walked out into the storm.